FARM FRIENDS

The Vet Visit

by Kimberly Derting & Shelli R. Johannes
illustrated by Kristen Humphrey

PICTURE WINDOW BOOKS
a capstone imprint

Published by Picture Window Books, an imprint of Capstone
1710 Roe Crest Drive, North Mankato, Minnesota 56003
capstonepub.com

Text copyright © 2025 by Kimberly Derting and Shelli R. Johannes
Illustrations copyright © 2025 by Capstone

All rights reserved. No part of this publication may be reproduced in whole or in part, or stored in a retrieval system, or transmitted in any form or by any means, electronic, mechanical, photocopying, recording, or otherwise, without written permission of the publisher.

Library of Congress Cataloging-in-Publication Data
Names: Derting, Kimberly, author. | Johannes, Shelli R., author. | Humphrey, Kristen, illustrator.
Title: The vet visit / by Kimberly Derting and Shelli R. Johannes ; illustrated by Kristen Humphrey.
Description: North Mankato, Minnesota : Picture Window Books, an imprint of Capstone, 2024. | Series: Farm friends | Audience: Ages 5–8. | Audience: Grades 2–3. | Summary: When a new foal is born at Poppy's family farm, the local veterinarian comes to make sure it, and all the other baby animals, are healthy.
Identifiers: LCCN 2023050924 (print) | LCCN 2023050925 (ebook) | ISBN 9781484695722 (hardcover) | ISBN 9781484695791 (paperback) | ISBN 9781484695869 (pdf) | ISBN 9781484695814 (kindle edition) | ISBN 9781484695807 (epub)
Subjects: LCSH: Animals—Infancy—Juvenile fiction. | Veterinarians—Juvenile fiction. | Farm life—Juvenile fiction. | CYAC: Animals—Infancy—Fiction. | Veterinarians—Fiction. | Farm life—Fiction.
Classification: LCC PZ7.D4468 Ve 2024 (print) | LCC PZ7.D4468 (ebook) | DDC 813.6 [E]—dc23/eng/20231229
LC record available at https://lccn.loc.gov/2023050924
LC ebook record available at https://lccn.loc.gov/2023050925

Design Elements: Shutterstock: MLeer

Designed by Elyse White

Printed and bound in China. 5827

Table of Contents

Chapter 1
Bella's Baby 7

Chapter 2
Dr. Herriot 12

Chapter 3
Animal Checkups 17

Chapter 4
A New Family Member 22

Welcome to the Farm!

Hi, I'm Poppy! I live on a farm. It's a lot of fun but also a lot of hard work. We grow vegetables, feed the animals, and make jellies from fruit.

My mom, dad, and little sister, Fern, all live on the farm too. So does my best friend, Vincent Van Goat.

Vincent is always butting in. When I feed the chickens, Vincent chases them away. When I pick the vegetables, Vincent kicks over the basket.

Playing with Vincent is even harder. He's always hungry! When I jump in the hay, Vincent tries to eat it. When I pick apples, Vincent tries to eat them. When I pack a picnic, Vincent tries to eat that too.

We have lots of animals to care for. There are pigs, chickens, horses, and cows. Come and see what it's like to live on a real farm!

Chapter 1
Bella's Baby

As soon as they finished morning chores, Poppy and Fern raced to the barn. They had been waiting for their horse Bella's new foal to arrive.

Mom and Dad were already in the barn. There was a new addition there too.

"Bella, you had your baby!" Poppy said.

"What should we name her?" Dad asked.

Poppy had lots of ideas. "How about Sweetie or Honey or Cookie?"

"I like Cookie!" Fern said.

"Do we need to get Cookie checked out?" Poppy asked. She loved when the local veterinarian came to the farm.

"Dr. Herriot is already on her way," Mom replied. "She'll examine Cookie and the other baby animals."

"Can we wait for her?" asked Poppy.

"Sure," Mom agreed.

Baaaa, Vincent said.

"Don't worry, Vincent. You can come too," Poppy said.

Chapter 2
Dr. Herriot

Soon, Dr. Herriot pulled up in her vet van. Her dog, Shep, was with her.

"Hi, girls!" Dr. Herriot said. "I hear you have a new family member."

"Bella had a baby!" Fern said. "We named her Cookie."

"We have one hundred and seven animals now," Poppy said.

Dr. Herriot grabbed her vet bag. "I can't wait to check out the new babies."

Poppy led Dr. Herriot to the horse barn and into the stall.

"What do you check?" she asked.

Dr. Herriot took out her stethoscope. "I have to examine Cookie's eyes, mouth, and ears," she said.

Poppy watched as the vet listened to Cookie's lungs, heart, and belly. She checked Bella too.

"Let's see if Cookie can stand," Dr. Herriot said.

They all watched as the foal stood. She wobbled a little but stayed on her feet.

Fern cheered. "She did it!"

Dr. Herriot patted Cookie's neck. "She looks strong to me," she said.

"Let's visit the other baby animals," Poppy said.

Chapter 3
Animal Checkups

Poppy and Fern walked

Dr. Herriot around the farm.

First, they visited Petunia's piglets.

"Wow!" Dr. Herriot said. "These babies have doubled in size since I was here last."

"When do they stop drinking milk?" Poppy asked.

"They will nurse for the next few weeks," Dr. Herriot said. "Then they can start having some solid foods."

Next, they stopped by the chicken coop. Dr. Herriot watched the chicks.

"They have bright eyes, fluffy feathers, and look very busy," she said. "Those are signs of healthy chicks."

Then, Dr. Herriot checked Minnie and her calf, Mickey. She also visited the ducklings and baby sheep.

"All of your animals look healthy," Dr. Herriot said. She gave Poppy and Fern each a sticker. "You've both done a great job."

"I want to be a veterinarian someday," Poppy said. "Then I can help take care of baby animals too!"

Chapter 4
A New Family Member

The vet was getting ready

to leave when Shep ran up.

He started barking.

"I think he wants us to follow him," Dr. Herriot said.

They followed Shep to the goat pen. A brown rabbit hid in the bushes.

"Do you think it might be hurt?" Poppy asked.

"Let me check," Dr. Herriot offered.

Poppy watched as the vet carefully picked up the rabbit. She examined its ears, legs, and belly.

"This rabbit isn't hurt,"
Dr. Herriot said. "She's going
to have babies."

Fern squealed. "Baby bunnies!
How many?"

"Rabbits can have up to
fourteen bunnies at a time,"
Dr. Herriot said.

Mom and Dad joined them.

"We should make her a safe space," Mom suggested.

"Let's set her up in this box until the babies come," Dad said.

Poppy and Fern made a soft bed using blankets and straw.

Dr. Herriot carefully moved the rabbit into the box.

"Our family is growing bigger every day," Mom said.

Poppy grinned. "A family can never be too big!" she said.

Glossary

calf (KAF)—a young cow

chick (CHIK)—a young bird

examine (ig-ZAM-in)—to check an animal to gather information about its health

foal (FOHL)—a horse that is less than one year old

nurse (NURSS)—to drink mother's milk

piglet (PIG-lit)—a baby pig

stall (STALL)—a compartment in a stable that houses a horse

stethoscope (STETH-uh-skope)—a tool used to listen to the heart and lungs

veterinarian (vet-ur-uh-NER-ee-uhn)—an animal doctor, also called a vet

Talk About It

1. Poppy wants to be a veterinarian someday. Do you think that would be a fun job? Why or why not?

2. Cookie got a checkup from Dr. Herriot. What did the vet have to examine on Cookie? Why was the checkup important?

3. While on the farm, Dr. Herriot visits a new foal, piglets, chicks, and a calf. What other animals do you think she might see?

Write About It

1. Poppy and Fern have lots of animals on their farm. Choose an animal from this story. Then write your own story—or a poem—about the animal you chose.

2. Imagine you're a baby animal on a farm, and Dr. Herriot is coming to visit. Write about your thoughts and feelings before, during, and after the vet visit.

3. Pretend you are a brand-new veterinarian. Write a letter about the animals you met and the things you did to make sure they were healthy. Remember to think about where the animals live, what they eat, and how to tell if they are healthy.

Did You Know? Baby Animal Facts

Baby animals have all sorts of different names, diets, and needs. Learn more about some of the animals that live on Poppy's farm!

Chickens

Baby chickens are called chicks. A newly hatched chick weighs about 1.5 ounces and is the size of its egg. Baby chicks eat grains, seeds, fruit and vegetable scraps, and mealworms.

Did You Know? Chicks imprint on the first large object they see, which is why mother hens stay nearby.

Cows

Baby cows are called calves. Most calves weigh 65 to 90 pounds (30 to 41 kilograms) when born. Calves get most of their nutrition from milk.

Did You Know? Calves start to "moo" shortly after birth.

Horses

A baby horse is called a foal. A newborn foal weighs about 100 pounds (45 kg) at birth. Foals drink their mother's milk. After about 10 days, they start to eat a bit of grass and hay.

Did You Know? Foals tend to be born at night. They can stand within two hours.

Pigs

Baby pigs are called piglets. At birth, most piglets weigh 3.5 to 4.5 pounds (1.6 to 2 kg). Piglets need milk every 30 to 60 minutes during the day and every four to six hours at night.

Did You Know? Newborn piglets learn to run to their mothers' voices. They can recognize their own names by the time they're 2 weeks old!

Rabbits

Baby rabbits are called kits or kittens. At birth, they weigh 1 to 1.5 ounces. Kits drink milk for their first 10 days. After that, they can start nibbling on small amounts of hay and veggies.

Did You Know? Kits are born completely blind. Their eyes open at around 10 days old.

About the Authors

photo credit: Vania Stoyanova

Kimberly Derting is an award-winning author of young adult novels as well as the coauthor of *Penny, the Engineering Tail of the Fourth Little Pig* and the popular Cece Loves Science picture book series. In college, Kimberly studied biology, but her real experiments are done at home, where she wrangles three kids, one husband, two dogs, a cat, and a rabbit named Thumper. You can visit her at kimberlyderting.com.

photo credit: Robin Mellom

Shelli R. Johannes is the author of *Shine Like a Unicorn*, the Theo Thesaurus series, and *Florence Nightingale*, a chapter book in Chelsea Clinton's She Persisted series. Shelli is also the coauthor of *Penny, the Engineering Tale of the Fourth Little Pig* and the Cece Loves Science picture book series. She lives in Atlanta, Georgia, with her British husband, two teens, two needy Goldendoodles, and one super sassy bird. You can visit her at srjohannes.com.

About the Illustrator

Kristen Humphrey grew up in a small town in southeastern Texas. She has always shared her home with many different animals, all of which have heavily influenced her artwork. While studying visualization at Texas A&M University, Kristen became interested in children's book illustration. When she's not drawing, Kristen enjoys dog walking, hiking, and horseback riding.